j599.88
Z13b

DETROIT PUBLIC LIBRARY

3 5674 02732615 7

W9-BXS-582

BABY CHIMP

A Grosset & Dunlap **ALL ABOARD BOOK**®

AFZ8974-1

For my darling niece, Jessica Cara—D.M.Z.

For Paris—B.O.

Special thanks to Colleen McCann, Ph.D., Assistant Curator of Primates, International Wildlife Conservation Park (Bronx Zoo).

Text copyright © 1996 by Debra Mostow Zakarin. Illustrations copyright © 1996 by Betina Ogden. All rights reserved. Published by Grosset & Dunlap, Inc., which is a member of The Putnam & Grosset Group, New York. ALL ABOARD BOOKS is a trademark of Grosset & Dunlap, Inc. Registered in U.S. Patent and Trademark Office. THE LITTLE ENGINE THAT COULD and engine design are trademarks of Platt & Munk, Publishers, which is a division of Grosset & Dunlap, Inc. GROSSET & DUNLAP is a trademark of Grosset & Dunlap, Inc. Published simultaneously in Canada. Printed in the U.S.A.

Library of Congress Cataloging-in-Publication Data

Zakarin, Debra Mostow.
    Baby chimp / by Debra Mostow Zakarin ; illustrated by Betina Ogden.
        p.   cm. — (A Grosset & Dunlap all aboard book)
    Summary: Describes the activities of a young chimp and her mother living in central Africa.
        1. Chimpanzees—Infancy—Juvenile literature.   2. Chimpanzees—Behavior—Juvenile literature.
    3. Parental behavior in animals—Juvenile literature.   [1. Chimpanzees.   2. Animals—Infancy.]   I. Ogden, Betina, ill.   II. Title.   III. Series.   QL737.P96Z34 1996
    599.88'44—dc20   95-51023
                                                                                                         CIP
    ISBN 0-448-41251-9   AC
    A   B   C   D   E   F   G   H   I   J

CL
9/98

BABY CHIMP

By Debra Mostow Zakarin
Illustrated by Betina Ogden

Grosset & Dunlap, Publishers

Deep in a forest in central Africa, the sun is just beginning to peek through the trees. As it rises, the animals who live here wake up—colorful birds, tiny tree frogs, leopards, wild pigs…and a group of chimpanzees. It is time for them to begin their day.

High in a tree, a mother chimp and her baby are just getting up. The baby chimp climbs out of her nest and swings to the ground. She uses her hands and feet to grab the branches as she goes.

When she gets to the ground, the baby chimp jumps up and down. "Hoo-hoo!" she calls. She wants her mother to hurry up. The rest of their group has already gone to find breakfast.

Chimpanzees live in groups of as many as one hundred. They travel through the jungle and sleep together, but they split into smaller groups to look for food.

Chimpanzees feed mainly on fruit and leaves, but they also like to eat nuts and seeds, tree bark, insects, and eggs. Now and then, they even hunt small mammals such as monkeys, young pigs, and rodents.

The baby chimp and her mother set off to find their breakfast. The baby climbs onto her mother's back. It is her favorite way to travel.

This baby chimp is one year old. She will stay close to her mother until she is about six.

Soon the mother chimp finds a big mound of dirt rising out of the grass. This looks like a good place to get breakfast. She picks up a long, thin twig. This will be her "fishing pole."

What could this mother chimp possibly be fishing for with a twig in a mound of dirt?

The mother chimp is fishing for termites!

The baby looks closely as her mother pokes the twig into the termite tunnel, then slowly pulls it out. It is crawling with termites! The mother chimp picks them off with her lips one by one.

The baby chimp is still too young to fish for termites by herself. But she watches carefully to learn how it is done.

Besides using twigs as "fishing poles," chimpanzees use other "tools" like rocks to crack nuts and open fruit. They are one of the few animals besides humans that are smart enough to make tools.

Chimpanzees belong to the great ape family, along with gorillas and orangutans. But chimps are more like humans than other apes.

gorilla

chimpanzee

orangutan

Like people, chimps are very social animals. The other chimps in their group are very important to them.

When the mother chimp hears a sound, she stands up and looks around. It is another family. The chimps greet each other with hugs and kisses and excited greeting calls.

The baby chimp likes to play with her friends.

They hang from low branches and jump up and down.

They twirl around and around until they get dizzy.

They do somersaults.

Then they all get in a tickle fight and laugh and laugh.

While the babies play, their mothers keep a careful eye on them. Mother chimps are very protective. They are always ready to step in if playmates get too rough.

Plip-plop. Suddenly it starts to rain. Play time is over.

The baby chimp climbs into her mother's lap, where it is warm and dry. The mother chimp uses a large leaf to shield her own head from the rain. Then the chimps sit still waiting for the rain to end.

When the rain finally stops, the baby chimp is dry, but her mother is very wet. Still, there is one good thing about the rain....

The mother chimp picks up a leaf. Then, like a sponge, she squeezes fresh, cool water from the leaf into the baby chimp's mouth. The baby licks her lips and opens her mouth wider for another drink.

"Hoo-hoo-hoo!" A large male chimp stands up and shakes a tree and screams a warning to the others. There is danger nearby! A hungry leopard.

The baby chimp holds on tight as her mother races with the other chimps up a tall fig tree.

Safely out of the leopard's reach, the chimps wait in the fig tree for the big cat to move on. The leopard is too heavy to climb onto the thin branches where the chimps hide.

Now the baby is no longer frightened. She is much more interested in a midday snack!

Full of tasty figs, the chimps settle down for an afternoon nap. Some chimps stretch out lazily. But the baby chimp likes snuggling close to her mother even better.

After her nap, the baby chimp decides it is time to explore. It is always fun to see what the other chimps are doing.

A young chimp is eating some delicious-looking leaves. But he does not want to share. When the baby chimp reaches for some of his dinner, he pushes her away, and the baby starts to cry. Chimps do not shed tears, but they do whimper just like people when they cry.

A chimpanzee's face can show many emotions. An open mouth with no teeth showing means a chimp wants to play or cuddle.

Puckered lips mean a chimp is excited.

Closed eyes and an open mouth mean a chimp is upset.

Lips pulled back and teeth showing might look like a big smile. But this really means a chimp is scared.

The mother chimp hears her baby crying and is there in an instant. She is mad. No chimpanzee can push her baby!

She stands up tall. The young male chimp bows his head and looks away. He knows better than to argue with an angry mother.

The baby chimp and her mother head off to join a group of chimps in a grooming circle. Grooming is a very important part of the chimps' day. It helps them keep their long hair clean, and it is a way to make friends and say, "I like you."

The baby chimp tries to sit still as her mother gently picks dirt and leaves and bugs out of her hair. She likes all the attention. But sometimes grooming tickles!

The baby chimp is tired now. The sun is setting. It is time for bed. One by one, the chimps climb into the trees. The mother chimp picks out a cozy spot for herself and her baby. Then she twists some leaves and branches together to make a new nest for the night.

As the baby chimp closes her eyes, she listens to the chimps around her call out their good nights. "Hoo–hoo–hoo."

Good night, baby chimp.